Tomasino

A Child of Peru

by Hervé Giraud
photos by Jean-Charles Rey

02029

BLACKBIRCH PRESS
An imprint of Thomson Gale, a part of The Thomson Corporation

THOMSON
✳
GALE ™

FRASER SCHOOL

Detroit • New York • San Francisco • San Diego • New Haven, Conn. • Waterville, Maine • London • Munich

© Éditions PEMF, 2004

First published by PEMF in France as *Tomasino, enfant du Pérou*.

First published in North America in 2005 by Thomson Gale.

Thomson and Star Logo are trademarks and Gale and Blackbirch Press are registered trademarks used herein under license.

For more information, contact
Blackbirch Press
27500 Drake Rd.
Farmington Hills, MI 48331-3535
Or you can visit our Internet site at http://www.gale.com

Photo Credits: All photos © Jean-Charles Rey except pages 6, 7, 21 (inset), Corel Corporation; page 21 (right) © PhotoDisc; Table of Contents collage: EXPLORER/Boutin (upper left); François Goalec (upper middle and right); Muriel Nicolotti (bottom left); CIRIC/Michel Gauvry (bottom middle); CIRIC/Pascal Deloche (bottom right)

LIBRARY OF CONGRESS CATALOGING-IN-PUBLICATION DATA

Giraud, Hervé.
  Tomasino : a child of Peru / by Hervé Giraud.
    p. cm. — (Children of the world)
  ISBN 1-4103-0546-5 (hard cover : alk. paper)
  1. Peru—Juvenile literature. 2. Quechua children—Peru—Juvenile literature. I. Title. II. Series: Children of the world (Blackbirch Press)

  F3408.5.G57 2005
  985'.00498323—dc22

                                                        2005000705

Printed in the United States of America
10 9 8 7 6 5 4 3 2

Contents

Facts About Peru

Agriculture:	coffee, cotton, sugarcane, rice, wheat, potatoes, corn, plaintains, coca
Capital:	Lima
Government:	republic
Industry:	mining, oil, fishing, textiles, clothing, food processing
Land area:	494,210 square miles (1,285,216 square kilometers)
Languages:	Spanish (the official language), Quechua, and Aymara
Money:	the nuevo sol
Natural resources:	copper, silver, gold, oil, timber, fish, iron ore, coal, phosphate, potash, hydropower, natural gas, farmland
Population:	27,167,000
Religion:	Catholicism

Peru

Peru is a country in South America. It is called "the Land of the Incas." A land of jungles, Peru also has volcanoes. A chain of mountains stretches from north to south across the whole length of Peru and the South American continent. This mountain chain is called the Andes.

The Andes Mountains

The Andes is the longest chain of mountains in the world. It is 4,971 miles (8,000 kilometers) long and has numerous active volcanoes scattered throughout.

The Andes Mountains in Peru are very tall and rugged.

On the Road

Tomasino, a young Quechuan Indian, lives in an area called the White Mountains. It is in the middle of the country.

Frequent earthquakes destroy houses made of adobe, which are bricks made of a mixture of clay and straw.

To get back to his village from the sea, where the capital city of Lima is, Tomasino rides an old bus that travels on twisty, rough roads.

The Peruvians' good humor makes the trip enjoyable. So does the scenery. The mountains' snowy peaks go up more than 19,684 feet (6,000 meters).

Above: Pilar, Tomasino's mother, and his sister, Laura, leave to join the men in the fields. Laura carries the lunch. Her mother continues to spin wool on her spindle, even while she walks.

Left: The small fields, farmed by hand, contrast with the dryness of the mountains, where erosion keeps anything from growing.

Tomasino's Home

The bedding is left out to dry after a humid night.

In this region of high plateaus, the clouds pass over high in the sky. The climate is invigorating, and the sun shines throughout much of the year.

But in the rainy season, between November and April, rain and mud make life difficult. At this altitude, the clouds blanket the land and fog lasts all day.

Above: A family portrait: the parents, grandparents, six children, and the animals. Tomasino sits astride Melodia, his white horse and constant companion.

Left: Tomasino's parents, Ronaldo and Pilar. Women wear hats that indicate their status. Married women wear white hats, widows wear black hats, and young girls wear hats decorated with pink ribbons.

At School

In September, all children from six to twelve years old begin the school year.

The path to school is very steep. Without money to buy books, however, the childrens' book bags are not heavy.

A long steep path to get to school.

School lasts only half a day. All Tomasino needs is a notebook and a pencil to perfect his Spanish, the official language of Peru.

Although at school Tomasino learns Spanish, at home he speaks Quechua, the language of his ancestors.

Secondary school, after age twelve, is not required. Most children in rural areas do not go.

FRASER SCHOOL

A picnic in the shade. The lunch that Pilar brings gives a welcome break from the day's work.

Working in the Fields

The rainy season occurs in summer in Peru. The fields are hoed and weeded to get them ready for planting. The potatoes will be harvested in May.

Everyone participates in the work in the fields. While Ronaldo, Tomasino's father, turns over the earth, the girls irrigate and plant potato tubers.

The children absolutely refuse to be separated from their animals when they go to work in the fields—especially because to get there, they have to climb!

Peruvians grow more than 500 kinds of potatoes. They like them so much that they call them "papa."

The campesinos, or farmers, of the Andes live a simple and rustic life. The family owns only necessities. Working the land and raising animals allows them to buy these things.

Animal Love

Along with the house, two small horses are the most valuable things Tomasino's family owns. They are used for all the outings and all the chores.

Above: A real baby lamb is better than a stuffed animal. It is much softer and really bleats.

Tomasino's family is too poor to own a tractor. The fields are too steep to use a tractor. To do the work, the animals pull the plow. They also carry the heavy sacks of potatoes.

Right: The gentle family cow is less favored by the children. However, her milk nourishes the family, and Pilar takes very good care of her.

Inset: Between Tomasino's brother and his favorite little donkey, there is never any disagreement.

17

Tomasino, with the help of his sisters, takes apart and washes one of the beds from their house.

When there is no school, Tomasino helps out at home just as all Peruvian children do. Without running water, a furnace, or electricity, the life of people in the Andes is the same as it has been for centuries.

Getting water and gathering wood are a big part of the day around the pueblo, or village.

Domestic animals are truly part of the family.

There is no limit to the passion Peruvians have for football, or soccer. Even the smallest school has a playing field. The children get together to pay for a ball, and they take great care of it.

Food

Along with potatoes, two main foods eaten by Peruvians are peppers and corn.

The house has a beaten earth floor, smoke-blackened walls, and very little furniture. The evening meal is primarily made of boiled corn.

Peppers and corn are two common foods in Peru.

The regional specialty is roasted guinea pig, but it is only eaten on festival days. Beef or chicken is eaten for ordinary meals.

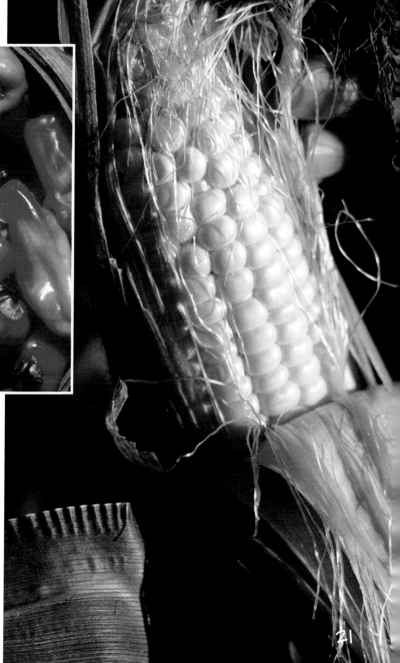

At the End of the Day

In spite of the harshness of the climate and many natural catastrophes, including earthquakes, mudslides, and avalanches, Tomasino wants to keep living here.

Without changing anything—or almost anything—from his ancestors' ways, Tomasino maintains a way of life that will guarantee him simple happiness and a good quality of life.

The immense beauty in front of his house explains the attachment the Indians have for their region—and their obvious joy of life.

Other Books in the Series

Arafat: A Child of Tunisia

Asha: A Child of the Himalayas

Avinesh: A Child of the Ganges

Ballel: A Child of Senegal

Basha: A Hmong Child

Frederico: A Child of Brazil

Ituko: An Inuit Child

Kradji: A Child of Cambodia

Kuntai: A Masai Child

Leila: A Tuareg Child

Madhi: A Child of Egypt

Thanassis: A Child of Greece